"Mommy, Mommy! Where are you?"

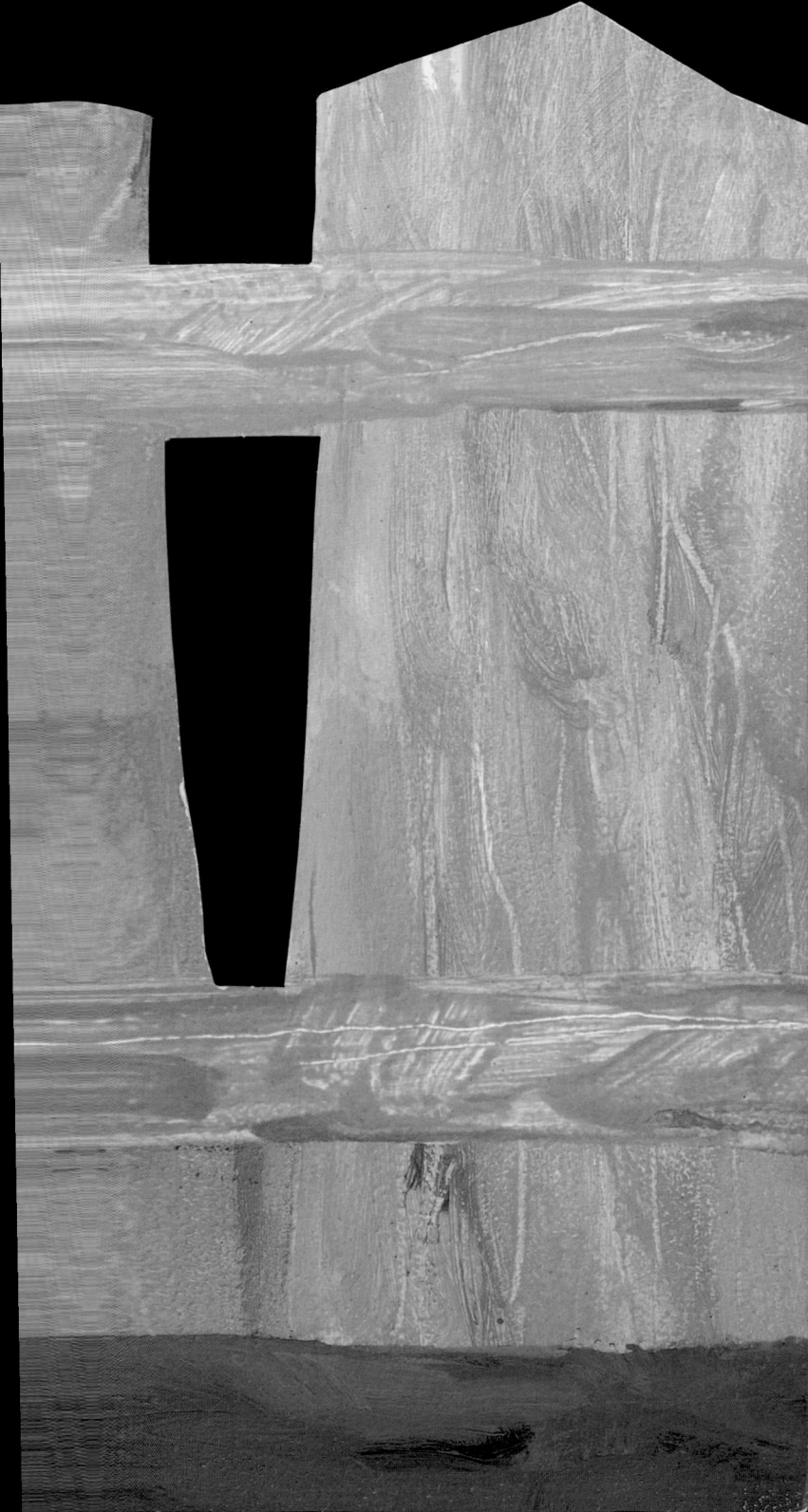

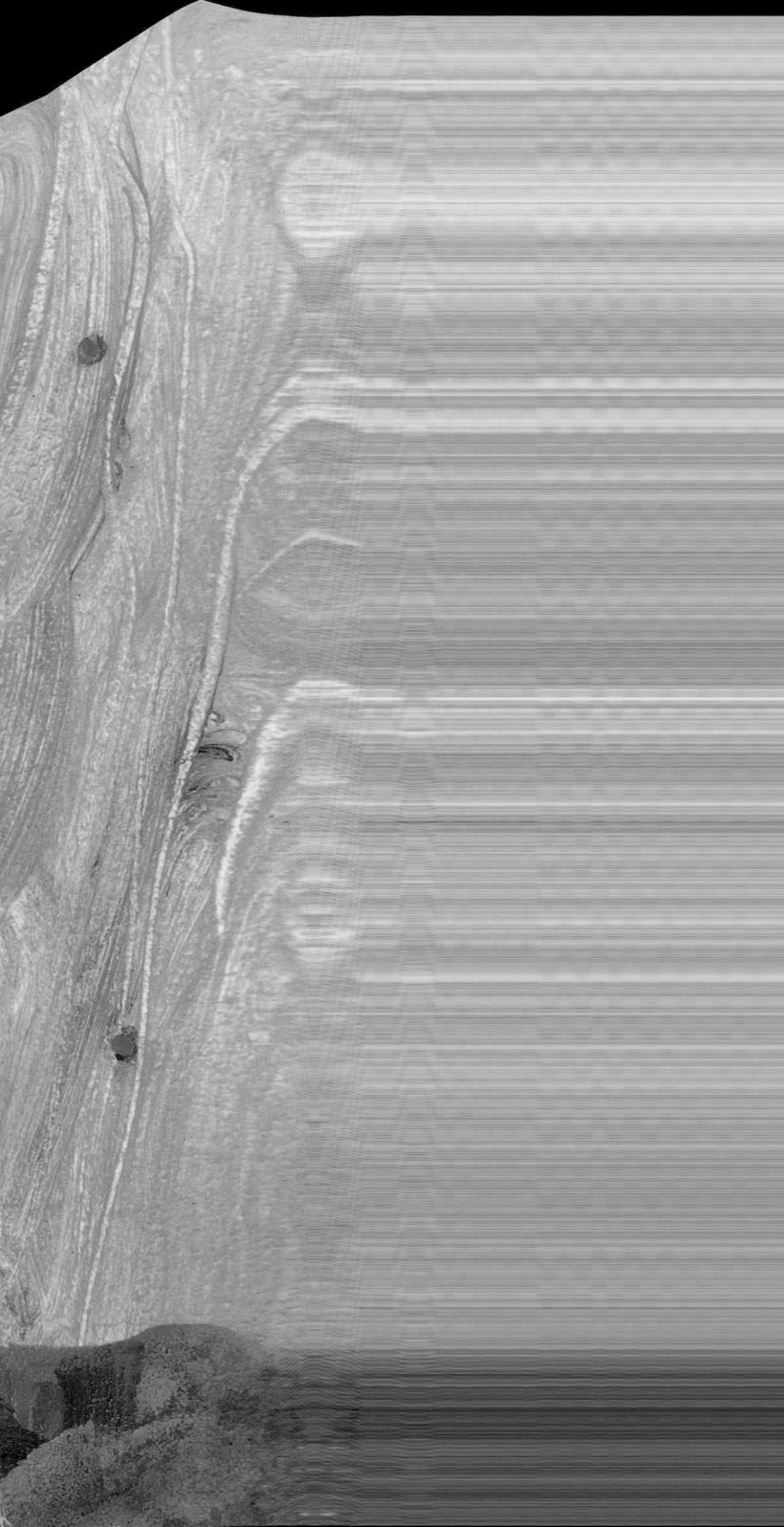

He ran to the big rock
where they liked to play.
"There you are!"

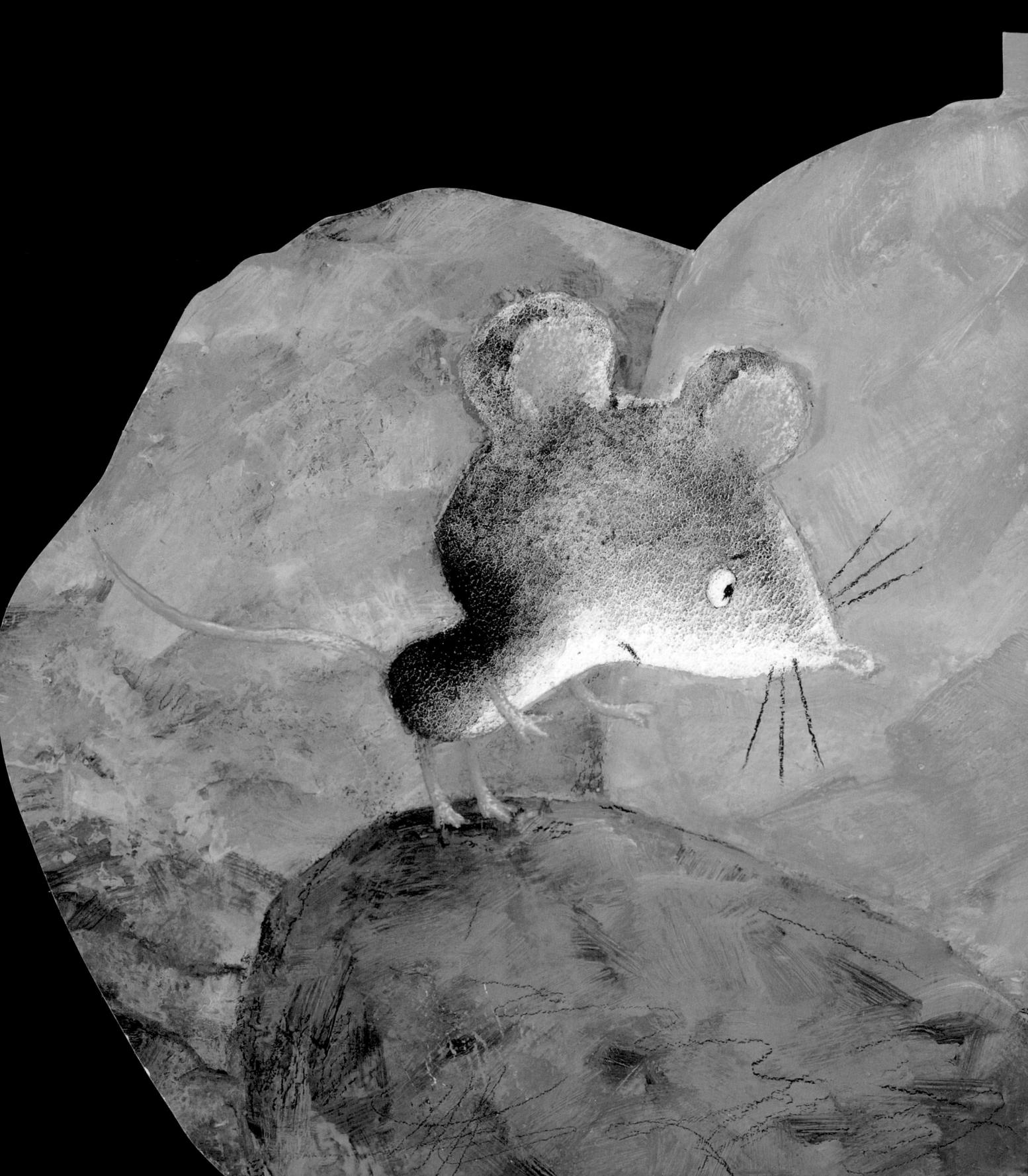

No, not Mommy.
Only an earthworm.

He ran to the garden
where they liked to smell flowers.
"There you are!"

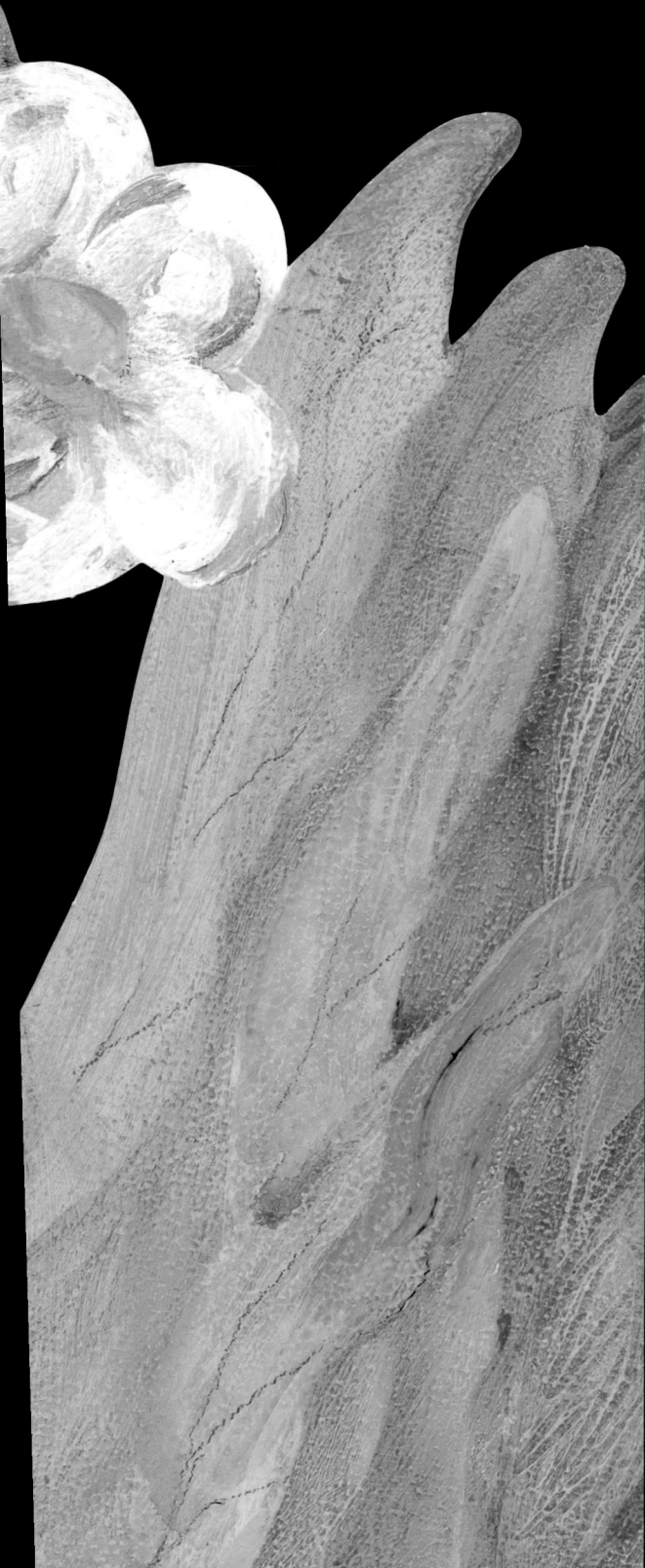

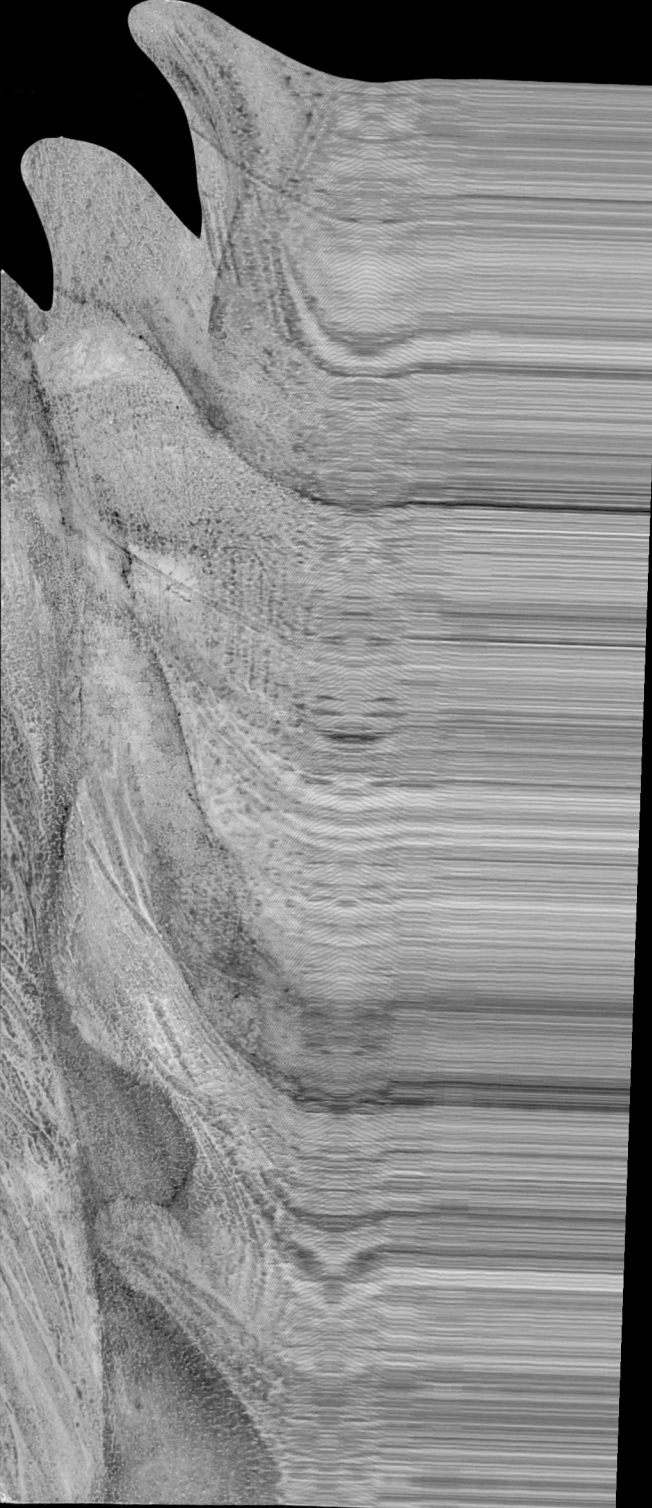

No, not Mommy.
Only a bunny.

He looked up
at the big tree
they liked to climb.
"There you are!"

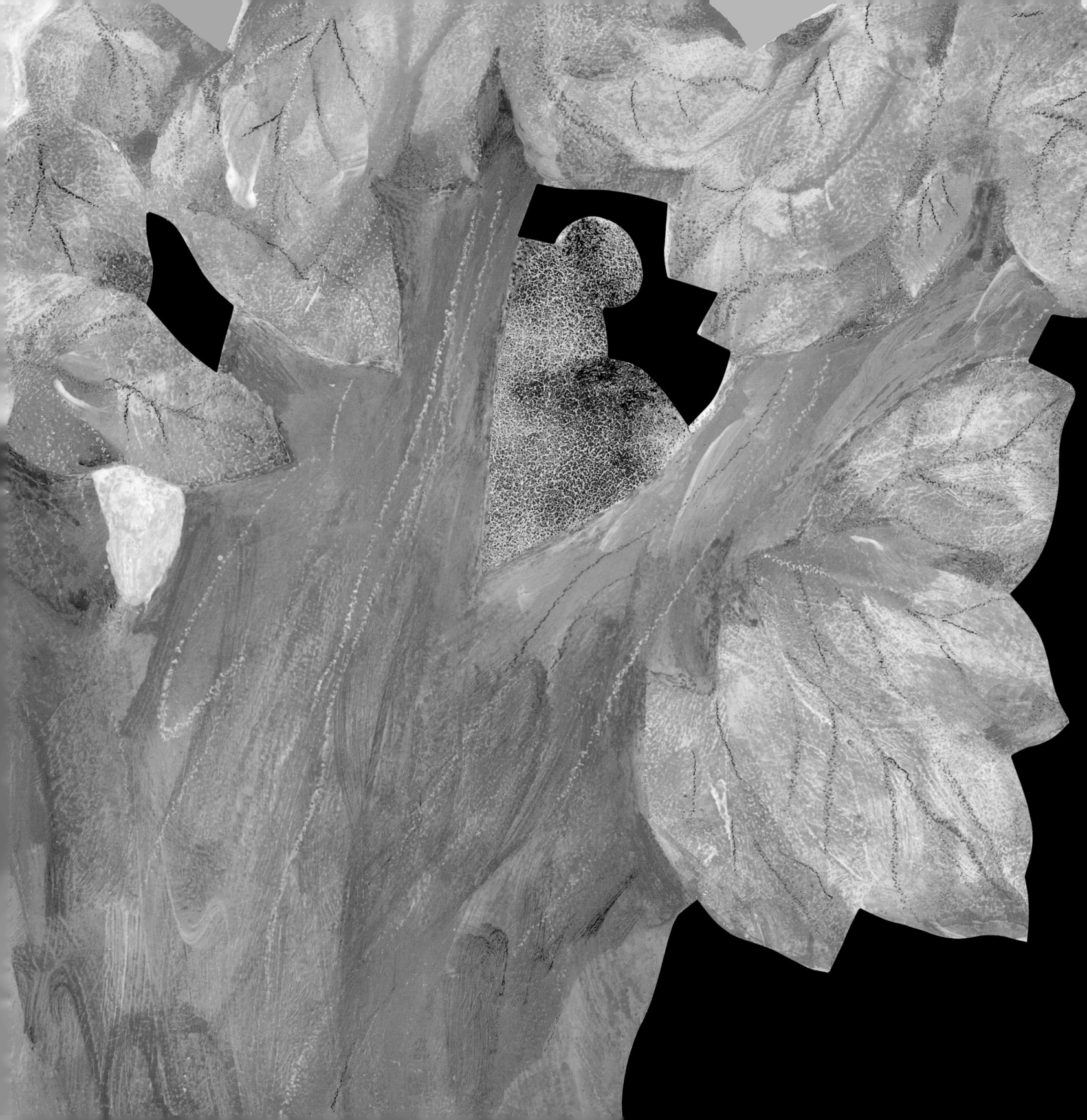

No, not Mommy.
Only a squirrel.

He ran to the lake where
they liked to splash.

"There you are!"

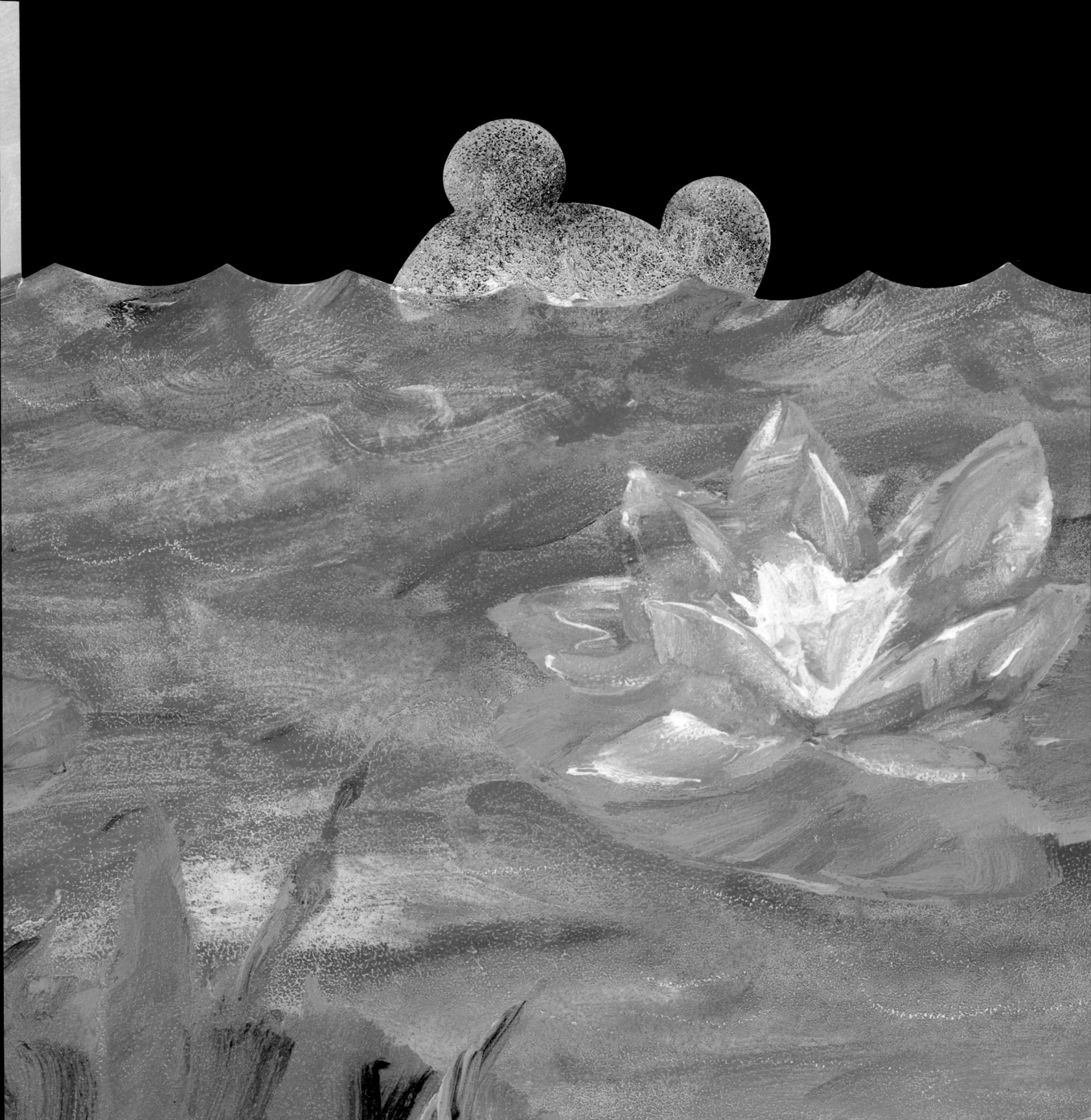

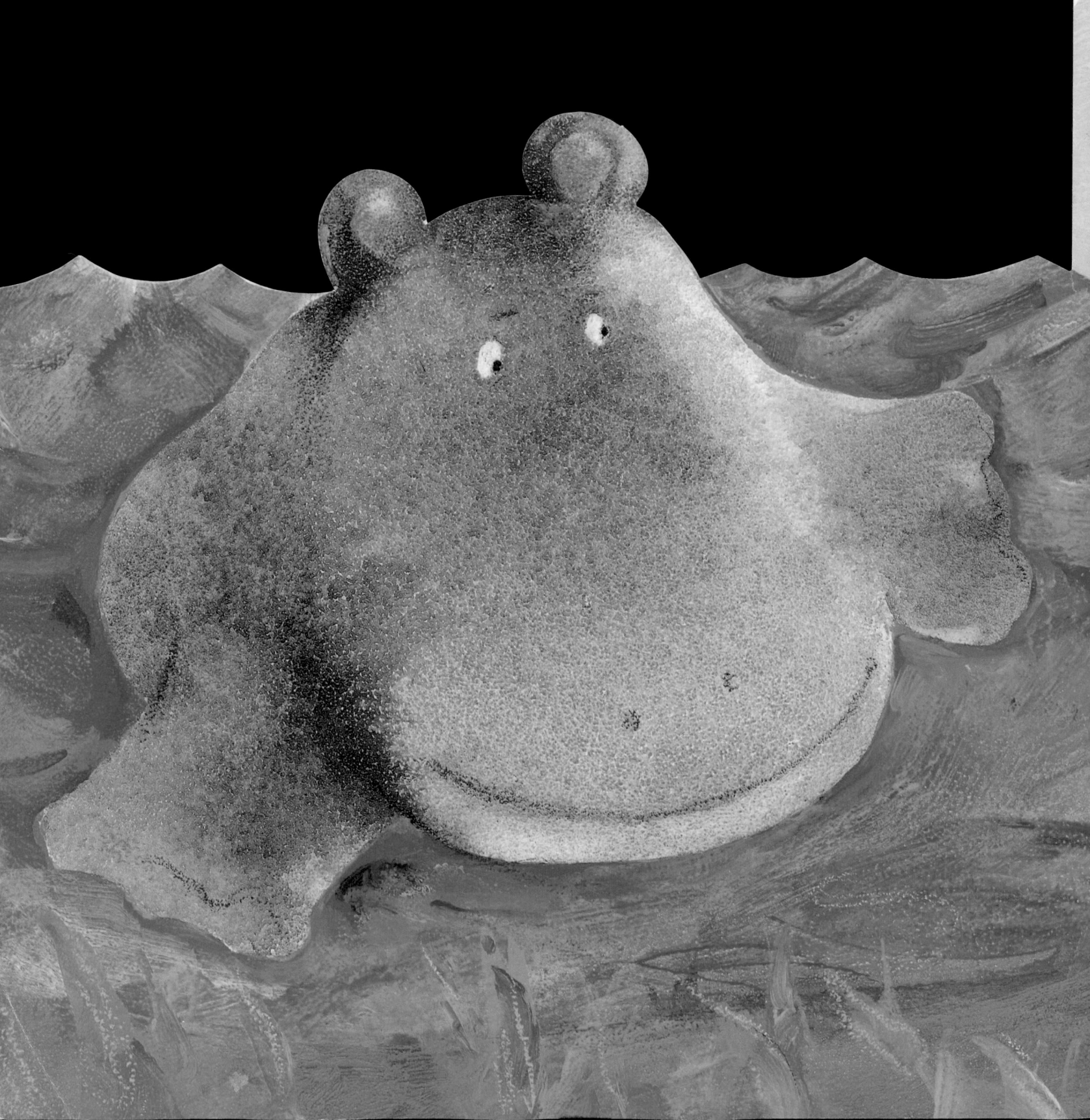

No, not Mommy at all!

Ozzy ran back to the garden.
There she was!

Those were
her whiskers
behind
the leaves.

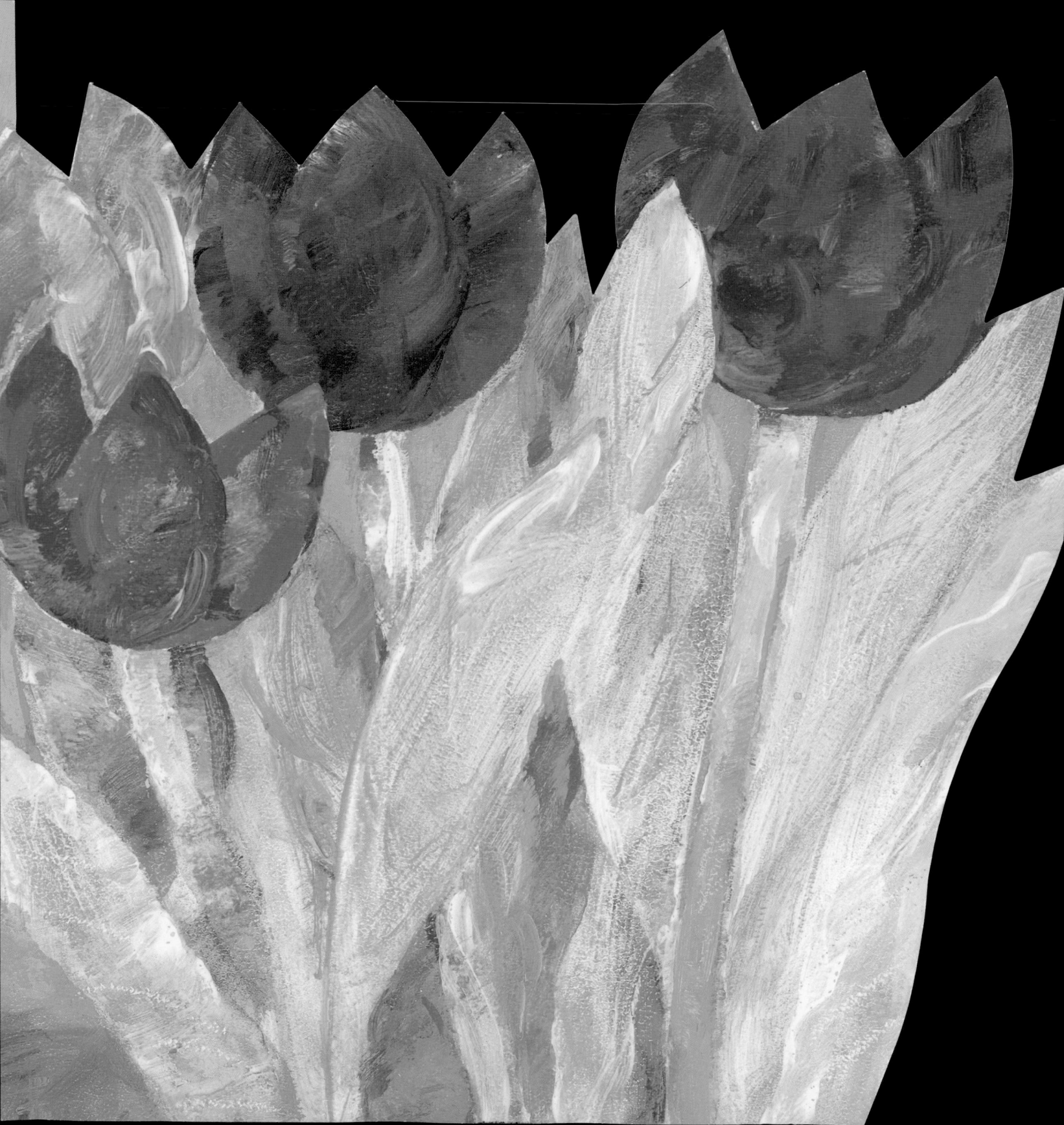

Ozzy ran as fast as he could, all the way home.
"MOMMY! MOMMY!
Where are you?"

And there she was!

"I was just getting breakfast for you," said Mommy. "Shall we eat now?"

So they did.

To my mom

Atheneum Books for Young Readers
An imprint of Simon & Schuster Children's Publishing Division
1230 Avenue of the Americas, New York, New York 10020
Copyright © 2009 by Leonid Gore
Book design by Ann Bobco
The text for this book is set in Adobe Garamond.
The illustrations for this book are rendered in acrylic paint on paper.
Manufactured in Malaysia
First Edition
2 4 6 8 10 9 7 5 3 1
Library of Congress Cataloging-in-Publication Data
Gore, Leonid.
Mommy, where are you? / Leonid Gore. — 1st ed.
p. cm.
"Ginee Seo Books."
Summary: A little mouse wakes up one day and, when he cannot find his
mother, goes in search of her.
ISBN-13: 978-1-4169-5505-4 * ISBN-10: 1-4169-5505-4
1. Toy and movable books—Specimens. [1. Mice—Fiction.
2. Mother and child—Fiction. 3. Toy and movable books.] I. Title.
PZ7.G659993Mo 2009
[E]—dc22 2008025994